Adam's Island

William Marshall was born in Brisbane, Australia, in 1929. He spent five years in the Australian army during the war in the Pacific. At the end of the war he studied photo-engraving, then studied anatomy in evening courses in Sydney. In 1950 he left for Europe and settled in France, where for many years he did a cartoon for *France-Soir*. He is both author and illustrator of the books he does for The Child's World.

Adam's Island

A story written and illustrated by
William Marshall

THE CHILD'S WORLD
MANKATO, MINNESOTA

Adam lived with Grandma
in a house
near a duck pond.

In the middle of the duck pond,
there was an island.
Sometimes,
Adam went to stay on the island.

5

Because, sometimes,
Adam was naughty.
Then Grandma would get mad.

When Grandma was mad,
she would chase* Adam,
shaking a feather duster* at him.
But Adam
ran much faster than Grandma.

*This word explained on page 45, numbers 1 and 2.

Adam jumped onto the island
in the middle of the duck pond.
Grandma couldn't get him.

There Adam waited
until Grandma calmed down.
One day he thought,
"You know what I need?
I need something to sit down on."

So the next time
Grandma got mad,
Adam didn't forget to bring along
his little red chair.

But he was still out of luck!
Adam had something to sit on,
but he didn't have an umbrella.

17

A little while later,
Adam was chased
by Grandma.
He didn't forget to
bring his yellow umbrella.

He thought,
"This is perfect.
Except life is a little monotonous.*
I should have brought my fishing rod."

*This word explained on page 46, number 3.

The next time, Adam ran quickly
to the island.
The fishing line got tangled
around his tail
and tripped him.

Adam fell into the middle of the pond.
The water splashed.
Adam yelled,
"Help, I don't know how to swim!"

Grandma put down her
pink feather duster
and she pulled Adam out of the pond
with the fishing pole.

Adam took off his wet clothes
and Grandma put them
next to the fireplace to dry.

Grandma said,
"You are going to stay in your bed."
Adam sniffled.

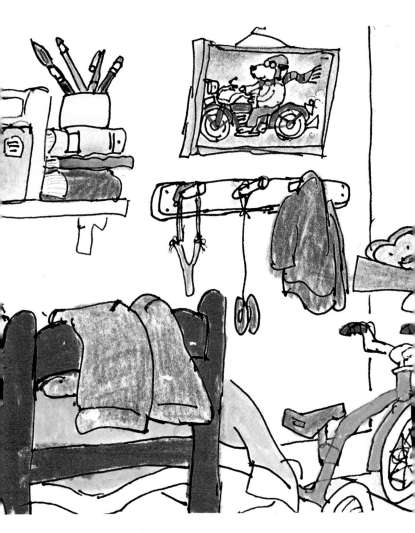

Grandma said,
"You are going to drink good hot soup."
Adam sniffled again.

When Adam was well again,
he undertook* building something
on his island.

*This word explained on page 46, number 4.

He secretly worked on it.
It was going to be a wonderful surprise
for Grandma.

Meanwhile, in the kitchen,
Grandma lit the oven
and stirred around in the pots.

She secretly worked on something.
It was going to be a wonderful surprise
for Adam.
Grandmama hid it in the tea canister.

Adam had made a bridge
for Grandma.
Grandma had baked
lots of pastries* for Adam.
They were both very happy with their
surprises.

*This word explained on page 47, number 5.

So they sat under
the yellow umbrella
to fish

while eating pastries. And this time,
they had everything they needed
on the island.

WORDS FROM THE STORY

1. **To chase** someone is
to run after them
in order to catch them.

2. **A feather duster** is a
kind of light small broom
made out of feathers,
used to remove dust
from fragile objects.

3. When nothing changes, when it's always the same,
we say that this is **monotonous**.

4. **To undertake** something is to start a project that might be long and difficult.

5. **Pastries** are
wonderful little tarts and cakes.

English edition copyright © 1993 by The Child's World, Inc.
123 South Broad Street, Mankato, Minnesota 56001
French edition copyright © 1990 Bayard Presse
All rights reserved. No part of this book may be
reproduced or utilized in any form or by any means
without written permission from the Publisher.
Printed in France.

Library of Congress Cataloging-in-Publication Data

Marshall, William, 1929-
    Adam's island / written and illustrated by William Marshall. p. cm.
    Summary: When Grandma gets mad at Adam, he jumps onto an island
in the middle of a duck pond; but, one day he falls into the water and needs
his grandmother to rescue him.
    ISBN 0-89565-889-5
    [1. Grandmothers – Fiction.   2. Islands – Fiction.]   I. Title.
PZ7.M356752Ad   1992
[E] – dc20   91-45912
                                             CIP
                                             AC